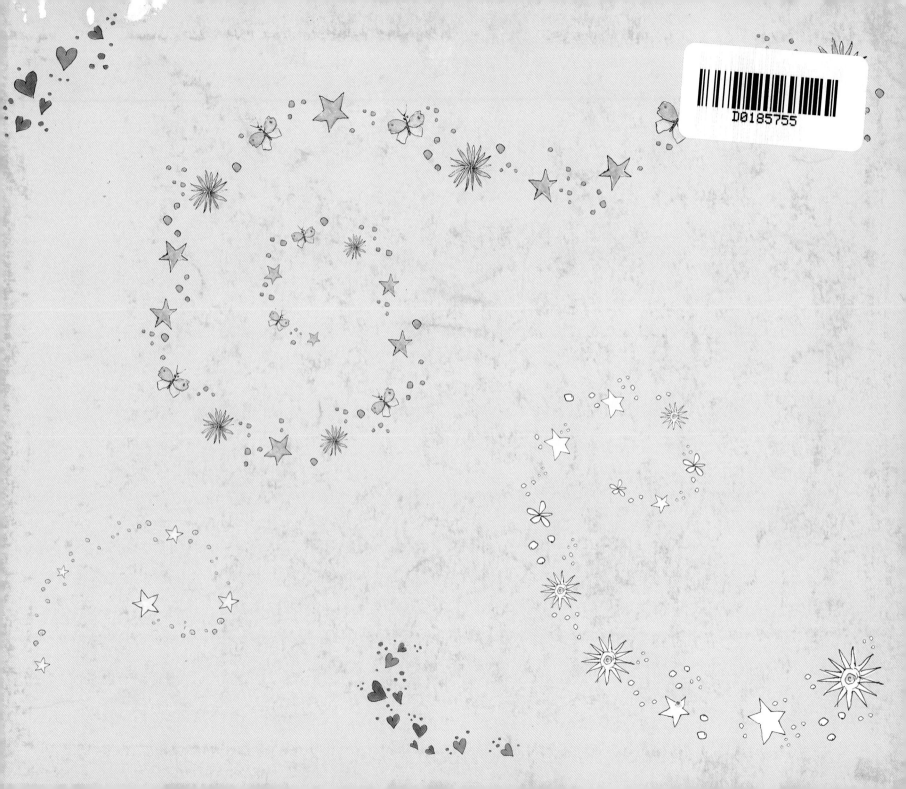

To little Angelina Ballerinas everywhere, and their parents and teachers   KH

To Carol Heaton, with love, thanks and appreciation of all you do for me   HC

PUFFIN BOOKS

Published by the Penguin Group
Penguin Books Ltd, 80 Strand, London WC2R 0RL, England
Penguin Putnam Inc., 375 Hudson Street, New York, New York 10014, USA
Penguin Books Australia Ltd, 250 Camberwell Road, Camberwell, Victoria 3124, Australia
Penguin Books Canada Ltd, 10 Alcorn Avenue, Toronto, Ontario, Canada M4V 3B2
Penguin Books India (P) Ltd, 11 Community Centre, Panchsheel Park, New Delhi – 110 017, India
Penguin Books (NZ) Ltd, Cnr Rosedale and Airborne Roads, Albany, Auckland, New Zealand
Penguin Books (South Africa) (Pty) Ltd, 24 Sturdee Avenue, Rosebank 2196, South Africa

Penguin Books Ltd, Registered Offices: 80 Strand, London WC2R 0RL, England

www.penguin.com

First published 2003
7 9 10 8 6

Set in Goudy

Made and printed in Malaysia by Tien Wah Press (Pte) Ltd

British Library Cataloguing in Publication Data
A CIP catalogue record for this book is available from the British Library

ISBN 0–670–91332–4

This edition produced for The Book People Ltd, Hall Wood Avenue, Haydock, St Helens, WA11 9UL

To find out more about Angelina, visit her web site at
www.angelinaballerina.com

Angelina Ballerina's
Invitation to the Ballet

Story by KATHARINE HOLABIRD ❀ Illustrations by HELEN CRAIG

TED SMART

One morning when Angelina skipped and hopped downstairs for breakfast, she found a large envelope waiting for her. "Who could it be from?" Mrs Mouseling asked with a smile.
Angelina recognized Miss Lilly's handwriting and couldn't wait to open it.

Miss Angelina Mouseling,
Vine Cottage,
Huckleberry Lane,
Chipping Cheddar,
MOUSELAND.

"I can't believe it! I've won two tickets to see Serena Silvertail at the Royal Ballet this Friday!" Angelina was so excited she pirouetted three times around the kitchen table.

"I'm going to invite Alice!" Angelina shouted as she flew out the door.

Angelina raced as fast as she could to Alice's house, but when she got there, Alice had already received a surprise of her own.

Miss Alice Nimbletoes,
56 Corncob Road,
Chipping Cheddar,
Mouseland.

T he twins didn't invite me to their stupid secret birthday!" Angelina sniffed. "But I don't care – I've just won two tickets to the *Cindermouse* ballet on Friday. Will you come with me, Alice?"

"Oh dear, Angelina," Alice groaned. "I wish I could, but I just told the twins I'll be at their party."

"Oh no!" cried Angelina.

"I'm very, very sorry," Alice whispered tearfully. Angelina gave her best friend a hug. "I'll have to go without you," she said bravely, "but I'm sure William would love to see Serena Silvertail dance."

Angelina waved goodbye and raced off to look for William. She found him down at Miller's Pond mucking about with boats.

"William, can you come with me to the Royal Ballet on Friday?" asked Angelina eagerly.

"Crumbs, Angelina," said William, shaking his head. "I promised to help Sammy out on Friday."

William pulled a scruffy envelope out of his pocket and showed it to her.

WILLIAM LONG TAIL,
RAILROAD CROSZING COTTAGE,
CABBAGE Street,
CHIPPING CHEDDAR.

1st Class Mail

12

Miss Angelina Mouseling,
The Royal Ballet School,
15 Queen Seraphina Square,
EDAMVILLE,
Mouseland.

ngelina shrugged. "Well, at least there's always Henry," she sighed, and she went off to find her cousin at the village playground. "Come and swing with me!" Henry cried when he saw Angelina. But Angelina didn't feel like swinging. She showed Henry and Aunt Lavender the ballet tickets.

"Please could Henry come with me?" Angelina asked.

"Oh yes!" Henry shouted.

"What a pity," said Aunt Lavender. "Henry's got an appointment with Dr Tuttle that afternoon."

Henry Mouseling

5 The Burrows

Chipping Cheddar

Mouseland

ngelina's tail drooped as she walked home sadly. She didn't want to go to the *Cindermouse* ballet without a friend, but who else could she invite?

Just then, Miss Lilly came rushing down the street.
"I've been looking everywhere for you!" she exclaimed. "Something quite extraordinary has happened," and she handed Angelina a letter.

SPECIAL DELIVERY

Mlle Lilly Mousakova, Dip. MRBS

Miss Lilly's Ballet School

The Village Green

Chipping Cheddar

Mouseland

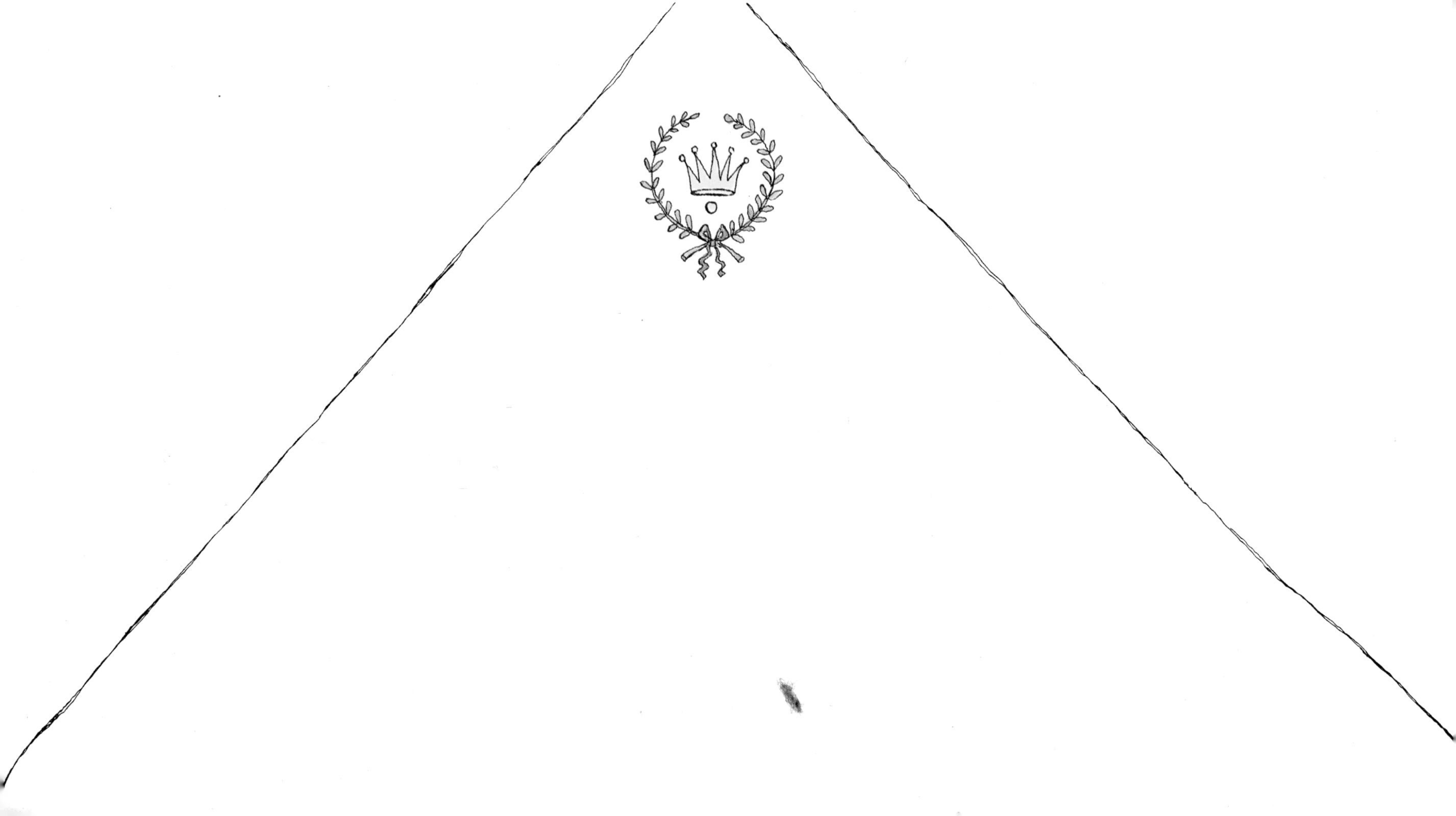

"What do you think, Angelina?" asked Miss Lilly. "Would you like to dance at the Royal Ballet?"

Angelina was already jumping up and down. "I can't wait!" she cried.

Mr and Mrs Mouseling were absolutely amazed when they saw Mr Operatski's letter. "And now I can invite you to the ballet!" said Angelina as she proudly gave them the two tickets. "We wouldn't miss this show for anything," smiled her parents.

The very next day when Angelina arrived at the Royal Ballet she immediately began rehearsing the Cindermouse Waltz. She had to work very hard to learn all of the steps.

Before she knew it, it was time for the Gala Performance. Angelina began to feel nervous. After all, she was about to dance with the best ballerina in Mouseland! Just then, Mr Operatski dashed into the dressing room. "This has arrived for you," he said, handing Angelina an envelope.

In the envelope was a lovely card and a wonderful surprise.
"A lucky charm – just what I need!" Angelina was so delighted
she twirled out the door. "I'm ready!" she called.

As Angelina waltzed onstage at Cindermouse's ball, her lucky charm sparkled in the spotlight. Dancing with Serena Silvertail was so exciting that she forgot to be nervous – in fact, she loved every minute.

"This has been the most exciting day of my life," Angelina sighed as she snuggled in her mother's lap on the train ride home. "I must be the luckiest mouseling in the whole of Mouseland!" Then Angelina yawned two huge yawns and soon she was fast asleep, dreaming of dancing at the Royal Ballet.